Barefoot

STUDY GUIDE

Sharon Garlough Brown

IVP Books

An imprint of InterVarsity Press
Downers Grove, Illinois

InterVarsity Press
P.O. Box 1400, Downers Grove, IL 60515-1426
ivpress.com
email@ivpress.com

InterVarsity Press® is the book-publishing division of InterVarsity Christian Fellowship/USA®, a movement of students and faculty active on campus at hundreds of universities, colleges, and schools of nursing in the United States of America, and a member movement of the International Fellowship of Evangelical Students. For information about local and regional activities, visit intervarsity.org.

All Scripture quotations, unless otherwise indicated, are taken from The Holy Bible, New International Version®, NIV®. Copyright © 1973, 1978, 1984, 2011 by Biblica, Inc.™ Used by permission of Zondervan. All rights reserved worldwide. www.zondervan.com. The "NIV" and "New International Version" are trademarks registered in the United States Patent and Trademark Office by Biblica, Inc.™

Cover design: Cindy Kiple
Interior design: Daniel van Loon
Images: woman: © Mark Owen / Trevillion Images
 row of bare feet: © kzenon/iStockphoto

ISBN 978-0-8308-4654-2 (print)
ISBN 978-0-8308-7083-7 (digital)

Printed in the United States of America ∞

InterVarsity Press is committed to ecological stewardship and to the conservation of natural resources in all our operations. This book was printed using sustainably sourced paper.

P	22	21	20	19	18	17	16	15	14	13	12	11	10	9	8	7	6	5	4	3	2
Y	38	37	36	35	34	33	32	31	30	29	28	27	26	25	24	23	22					

Contents

Introduction

Many readers of *Barefoot* have requested a guide for exploring the spiritual formation themes within the novel and for processing the characters' journeys with God and each other. In response, I'm delighted to provide this study guide as a resource for individuals and groups.

Here you'll find twelve weeks of daily Scripture reading, reflection questions, and invitations to prayer. Some weeks you'll have five days of reflection questions with the sixth day designated as a review day. Other weeks days five and six will both provide opportunities for prayerful review. At the end of each week you'll also find spiritual disciplines you may wish to incorporate more intentionally into your life with God, and group discussion questions and exercises to explore and practice in community.

You can decide whether to read *Barefoot* first in its entirety and then return to do a slow study with the guide, or whether to read it a section at a time, matching your pace to the daily questions. I do recommend keeping a travelogue of your journey. Even if you aren't in the habit of using a journal, you'll benefit from having a record of what you're noticing as you move forward.

Not every question will resonate with you. That's okay. You don't need to answer every question every day. But do watch for any impulse to avoid a question because it agitates you or makes you feel uncomfortable. That's probably the very question you need to spend time pondering! If you don't have time to answer the questions you want to reflect on, simply mark them and return on the review days. If something in the chapter speaks to you and isn't addressed in a question, spend time journaling and praying about it.

The daily Scripture texts echo the themes of the daily readings from the book. I recommend reading the Scripture first so that the Word shapes and frames your pondering.

I pray you'll encounter God in significant ways as you read, reflect, and pray. May you find many opportunities to remove your shoes and worship on holy ground.

Sharon Garlough Brown

Reading for Week One: Chapter One

....

Week One: Day One

CHAPTER ONE: MEG (PP. 11-16)

Scripture: Psalm 62:1-8

1. What words or images come to mind when you hear the word *resilient*? What does it mean to be resilient in hope?

2. Meg tells Hannah she often has "imaginary conversations with people who aren't here" (p. 13). What kinds of conversations or voices typically play in your head? Spend time offering these voices to Jesus and hearing his words of truth.

3. Both Meg and Hannah struggle to be on the receiving end of care. Why? How practiced are you at receiving love and care from others? If it is hard for you to receive, why might this be?

4. "Even with everything [Meg] had seen about God's faithfulness, even with everything she'd experienced the past few months about God's

presence and love, she still found it hard to trust. So that's what she was learning to offer—the truth. To God. To others. To herself. No denying her fears. No stuffing her sorrow. All the anxiety and the heartache, the regret and the guilt, the longings and the desires, the wrestling and the sin, the past and present and future—all of it belonged at the feet of Jesus. All of it" (p. 15). What are you learning to offer to Jesus? What do you need courage to see?

5. The Spirit's echoing word for Meg is *hope*. Is there any particular word or theme echoing for you? If nothing immediately comes to mind, spend some time listening for one.

6. "For God alone my soul waits in silence, for my hope is from him" (Psalm 62:5 NRSV). Read this verse slowly several times. Does it describe your practice or your longing? What would it mean to wait in silence and with hope for God? Offer your response to God in prayer. Then spend time sitting in silence.

. . . .

Week One: Day Two

∞

CHAPTER ONE: *MARA* (PP. 17-22)

Scripture: Matthew 5:43-48

1. What family memories, traditions, or heirlooms are important to you? Why? Offer these to God with gratitude. If there are any that have been lost over the years, speak to God about the emotions that rise within you as you remember them.

2. What "gotcha games" are Mara and Tom playing? When are you tempted to retaliate or get even? Offer these impulses to God in prayer.

3. Bring to mind an occasion when you felt too angry to speak or too disappointed to cry. Is there anything unresolved to offer God in prayer?

4. Read Matthew 5:43-48 aloud several times. Bring to mind people who make life difficult for you. What is God's specific invitation to you? Journal your response.

....

Week One: Day Three

CHAPTER ONE: *HANNAH* (PP. 23-30)

Scripture: Psalm 127:1-2

1. When are you tempted or most likely to lose patience? Do you see any patterns? Which spiritual practice(s) could help counteract the gravitational pull toward impatience?

2. What kinds of stories are most likely to evoke your compassion? Why? How readily do you practice intercessory prayer, generosity, mercy, or serving others in need? Who is God calling you to serve in these ways?

3. "The slowing down, the paying attention, the deliberate rest and unplugging, the transition from the driven life to the received life—all of this was a paradigm shift [Hannah] still needed time to process and integrate" (p. 26). What about you? What's the pace of your life? In what ways can you practice the discipline of slowing down and paying attention today? Or, if you've been practicing like Hannah, what fruit do you see?

4. "By the faithful and stealthy work of the Spirit, Hannah had begun to perceive . . . all the ways her personal identity had been swallowed up and enmeshed with her professional one, all the ways she had defined herself by what she did for God rather than who she was to him—the beloved" (p. 27). Do you share anything in common with where Hannah has been or what she is perceiving? Offer what you notice to God in prayer.

5. How are you integrating play and rest into your rhythm of life?

6. Read Psalm 127:1-2 again several times. What is stirred in you as you read? Offer your response in prayer.

. . . .

Week One: Day Four

CHAPTER ONE: *CHARISSA* (PP. 31-40)

Scripture: Galatians 5:1

1. What does Charissa see at Crossroads? How does this affect her? Stir her to action?

2. Miss Jada tells the volunteers, "Everybody you meet is made in Abba's image. If you can't see it, look harder. Ask for new eyes" (p. 32). Is there anyone you have trouble seeing in this way? Why? Ask God for new eyes.

3. "By grace [Charissa] had begun to see . . . her socially acceptable forms of idolatry: her thirst for honor and recognition, her pursuit of excellence for her own sake, her deriving her sense of self not from her identity as the beloved in Christ but from her own achievements and reputation" (p. 36). What are your "socially acceptable forms of idolatry"? Spend some time confessing these to God in prayer and meditating on the identity Christ has given you.

4. How do you respond when others try to control or manipulate you through their expectations or even their gifts? Bring to mind an example of such a conflict and offer what you notice to God in prayer.

5. Why does Charissa think she needs a "less self-centered image of God"? What images of God are shaping your life with him right now?

6. Read Galatians 5:1 again. Where do you sense a gravitational pull toward slavery rather than freedom in Christ? Which practice(s) can help you resist that pull? What kind of freedom can you celebrate today?

....

Week One: Days Five and Six

REVIEW

These are days to revisit any reflection questions you weren't able to complete earlier in the week. Return to the Scripture passage that either most stirred you or least stirred you, and spend time meditating on it.

Spiritual disciplines to note from the characters' journeys in chapter one: waiting, generosity (both practicing and receiving), Scripture meditation, serving, rest, play, community, attentiveness

Week One Group Discussion

1. Discuss any points of resonance with the characters' journeys thus far. Who are you sympathetic or frustrated with? Why? In what ways are the characters providing windows to glimpse God and others more clearly, or mirrors to see yourself?

2. Choose one of the Scripture texts for the week for group lectio divina. (This spiritual discipline is described in chapter four of *Sensible Shoes*.) What's stirring for you as you prayerfully listen to the Word?

3. Which spiritual disciplines can you practice in community? Perhaps there's a mission agency that easily slips off the public radar during the year. Discuss creative ways to serve together.

4. How can the group pray for you as you move forward with hope?

Reading for Week Two:
Chapter Two

Week Two: Day One

CHAPTER TWO: MARA (PP. 41-46, 59-62)

Scripture: Isaiah 41:10

1. What are some of the difficult family dynamics you observe in Mara's life? Do you identify with her in any particular ways?

2. When Jeremy mentions being at Crossroads as a little boy, Mara shares a piece of her past with Kevin. Have you ever had the opportunity to divulge a piece of family history you hadn't widely shared before? What was the occasion? The response?

3. Mara is provoked by Miss Jada's response to the news of her divorce. How do you react to her warning about watching out for a root of bitterness? What about her insistence that Mara pray for God to rescue and save—not punish—Tom? Offer what you notice to God in prayer.

4. When Mara is startled awake by Brian's presence in her bedroom, a long-buried memory of trauma surfaces. If Mara divulged this trauma to you, how would you respond?

5. Are there any unresolved issues of trauma in your own life that need the wise and discerning companionship of others? Pray about what next steps God would invite you to take toward healing and restoration.

6. Read Isaiah 41:10 several times. Breathe each of the lines as prayer. In what ways is God making his presence, love, and power known to you?

....

Week Two: Day Two

∞

CHAPTER TWO: HANNAH (PP. 47-54)

Scripture: Romans 12:1-2

1. Thoughts of an adversary bringing upheaval encroach on Hannah as she plays with Nathan and Jake. Who has brought upheaval or disruption to your sense of equilibrium in life? How do you feel about him or her? Offer names or experiences to God in prayer.

2. Read the Wesley Covenant prayer (p. 52). Which lines catch your attention? Which are challenging to pray? Why?

3. Hannah writes that she's trying to "be in that place of 'holy indifference,' where [her] desire or hope is not in a particular outcome but in whatever brings God glory and honor and praise" (p. 53), but she's struggling.

Why? In what ways do you identify with her struggle to wholeheartedly yield all things to God?

4. "[Nathan] often says that his 'Here I am' prayer of surrender describes his intention, but not always his practice" (p. 54). Is *hineni* a word you are able to offer to God in trust? Why or why not?

5. Read Romans 12:1-2 again. Then offer your longings, fears, receptivity, and resistance to God in prayer.

....

Week Two: Day Three

CHAPTER TWO: *MEG* (PP. 55-58)

Scripture: Mark 10:13-16

1. Have you ever had a dream where the veil between this life and the next seemed thin? Would such an experience be a gift or a sorrow to you? Why?

2. As they view a "special display of glory," Hannah says to Meg, "It hits me sometimes, the wonder of being the only person in the world praising God for a particular gift of beauty, in a particular moment" (p. 56). Move

to a window or step outside. Look or listen carefully. What unique display of beauty catches your attention and invites you to give God praise?

3. At Hannah's suggestion Meg reads Mark 10:13-16 and tries to pray with her imagination. What is she trying to control as she prays? Does anything from her experience resonate with you?

4. Read Mark 10:13-16 and imagine yourself in the scene. What do you notice about Jesus? What do you need to receive from him? Offer what you notice to God in prayer.

···

Week Two: Day Four
~

CHAPTER TWO: CHARISSA (PP. 63-69)

Scripture: Luke 2:33-35

1. In what ways does the familiar story of the wise men come to life for Charissa as she listens to a sermon? Have you ever been surprised by a familiar story coming to life in a new way? How has your heart been pierced or revealed by the light of the Word?

2. What's pushing Charissa's buttons? In what ways do you identify or sympathize with her?

3. How do you respond when buried pain—either your own or someone else's—is flushed to the surface?

4. What do you notice about Charissa's response to Mara's story? How is it helpful? Unhelpful? Does this interaction stir any memories for you of being in either Charissa's or Mara's shoes? Is there anything for you to offer to God?

5. Read Luke 2:33-35 again. How has Simeon's prophecy about Jesus been fulfilled in your own life? What inner thoughts have been revealed by Jesus? Offer your response to God in prayer.

....

Week Two: Days Five and Six

CHAPTER TWO: REVIEW

Return to any questions you were not able to answer this week. Note in your journal any aha moments that need prayerful integration. Close your time of review by praying Wesley's prayer as honestly as you're able.

Spiritual disciplines to note from the characters' journeys in chapter two: journaling, discernment, praying for adversaries, intercessory prayer, Scripture meditation, praying with imagination, attentiveness, gratitude

Week Two Group Discussion

Use Mark 10:13-16 as a text for praying with imagination. Enter the scene as a participant. What do you see? Hear? Where do you find yourself in the story? Spend time in personal reflection, then discuss the experience together.

1. What (or who) inhibits your coming to Jesus? Listen to Jesus speak his welcome to you. How do you feel? Offer your response to God in prayer.

2. What blessing do you long to receive from Jesus? Name your longing to God in prayer.

3. Is there anyone you want to take to Jesus for a blessing? What words might he speak to them? To you? Imagine his hands on you and your loved ones. Savor the blessings spoken.

4. Who has brought you to Jesus for a blessing? Spend time thanking God for the ones who have taken you to him in prayer.

5. What most stood out for you in the time of personal reflection?

6. How can the group pray for you?

Reading for Week Three: Chapter Three

....

Week Three: Day One

∞

CHAPTER THREE: MEDITATION ON PSALM 131

Turn to the prayer exercise (pp. 72-73) and answer the personal reflection questions.

....

Week Three: Day Two

∞

CHAPTER THREE: MEG (PP. 74-77)

Scripture: Psalm 131

1. Which details from Meg's interaction with the text catch your attention? Why?

2. What helps you to calm and quiet your soul? Is community a blessing or a burden when you're upset?

3. How aware are you of the childhood experiences that affect your life with God? Spend some time talking with God about this.

4. As Meg contemplates what has been painful, she also remembers Mrs. Anderson's presence as a gift. What gifts has God given you in the midst of sorrows? Spend time naming these with gratitude to God.

5. What do you think of Mara's suggestion about writing a letter as a way to "dump the junk"? Are there any letters for you to write? To whom?

6. Read Psalm 131 again. What images catch your attention and invite you to linger today?

··

Week Three: Day Three

∞

CHAPTER THREE: *MARA* (PP. 78-87)

Scripture: Psalm 131

1. What is Mara pondering about Psalm 131? Is there a gap for you between knowing the "right response" and your honest response to questions about where you are with God? Talk with God about the gap.

2. Mara decides not to disclose to Meg and Hannah Tom's violation of her. Why? What do you think of her decision?

3. In what ways is Mara feeling stuck and trapped? Do you share anything in common with her?

4. Imagine yourself crawling into the lap of God to be embraced and soothed. What words might God whisper over you?

5. Read Psalm 131 again. Which words call to you? What's your response?

....

Week Three: Day Four

∽

CHAPTER THREE: *HANNAH* (PP. 88-93)

Scripture: Psalm 131

1. What is Hannah pondering after praying with Psalm 131? Do you share anything in common with her?

2. What's at the root of her wrestling over how much to say to her parents? Have you ever wrestled over how much truth to speak? What were the circumstances? How did you receive counsel about what to do?

3. What do you notice about Hannah's interaction with the member from Westminster? Is there anything that troubles you? Why?

4. Bring to mind some significant threshold moments in your life. How do you typically respond to such transitions?

5. Read Psalm 131 again. What is your soul like right now? Offer what you notice to God in prayer.

··

Week Three: Days Five and Six

∞

REVIEW

Return to any questions you were not able to answer this week. Note in your journal any aha moments that need prayerful integration. If you identified a letter to be written but haven't yet written it (day two), spend time composing it.

Spiritual disciplines: Scripture meditation, prayer, community, journaling, discernment, attentiveness

Week Three Group Discussion

1. Read Psalm 131 together. What most stood out to you in your time of personal reflection on this psalm this week?

2. Do you have any other aha moments to offer from the week?

3. Have an honest conversation about how much truth telling you're able to do in your group context. Is there anything that hinders deep authenticity and vulnerability? Any new commitments or renewal of commitments to make to one another?

4. Conclude by inserting your own names into the call to hope in Psalm 131:3: "O [name], hope in the LORD from this time forth and forevermore" (ESV). Pray for your fellow travelers to hope in the Lord from this time forth and forevermore.

Reading for Week Four:
Chapter Four

....

Week Four: Day One

CHAPTER FOUR: *CHARISSA* (PP. 94-98)

Scripture: Psalm 51:6-7

1. Kicking at accumulated snow and sludge becomes a metaphor for
    Charissa's longing. What do you desire to purge? In what ways do you
    need to be purged?

2. What is Charissa frustrated about? What frustrates you about your
    progress in the journey toward becoming more like Jesus?

3. What do you notice about John and Charissa's interaction with Reverend
    Hildenberg? With each other? Who are you more sympathetic with—
    John or Charissa? Why?

4. "Learn to linger with what provokes you." What's provoking you right
    now? Offer what you notice to God in prayer.

5. Read Psalm 51:6-7 again, speaking it as prayer.

....

Week Four: Day Two

CHAPTER FOUR: HANNAH (PP. 99-106)

Scripture: Zephaniah 3:17

1. Read Nathan's prayer for Hannah, making it a prayer for yourself: *Lord, let me know your presence, right in the midst of [name where you find yourself today]. Thank you for being with me as the Mighty One who saves. When I am agitated, quiet me with your love. Let me experience your delight in me today. Let me hear the joyful song you sing over me, and let me not resist your exuberance and abundance* (pp. 99-100).

2. Which parts of the prayer are hard for you to receive? Believe? Offer your resistance or doubt to God.

3. What helps you to embrace God's love and delight? In what ways are you tempted to shrink back from the abundance and exuberance of God's love? Offer your longings to God in prayer.

4. What do you notice about Hannah's parents? About her interaction with them? Does anything surprise you? Why?

5. What kind of conversation do you hope Hannah will be able to have with her parents? What does this reveal about your own longings in relationships?

6. Read Zephaniah 3:17 again. Spend time resting in God's love, joy, and delight.

....

Week Four: Day Three

∽

CHAPTER FOUR: MEG (PP. 107-112)

Scripture: Psalm 23:1

1. What observations do you make about Meg as she teaches? About Rachel when she enters unexpectedly? About the way they interact with one another?

2. In which relationships have you felt disregarded? What is God inviting you to do?

3. The sketch that Meg has hung on the door upstairs is *Jesus and the Lamb* by Katherine Brown. Find a picture of it online. How does the art speak to you? Offer your response to God.

4. Read Psalm 23:1. Recite it multiple times. Breathe it and pray it. What do the words mean to you? Talk with God about what you notice.

Week Four: Day Four

CHAPTER FOUR: SUMMARY

Scripture: Romans 12:18

1. Each of the characters is navigating challenges or conflict within relationships—with children, parents, spouses, or siblings. In your reflection and prayer time today, bring to mind the relationships that cause you stress or pain. Speak to God about each one, offering your hurts, confusion, longings, disappointment, and fears. What do you need from God?

2. Spend time praying for each of the people who make life difficult for you. How might the Lord desire to form you in the midst of these relationships?

3. Read Romans 12:18 several times. Which words or phrases catch your attention? Why?

4. What does it mean to "live peaceably" with others? What doesn't it mean? What is God inviting you to do? Offer your response in prayer.

....

Week Four: Days Five and Six

REVIEW

Where is God inviting you to linger? Go deeper? Return to the things that provoked you this week and watch for the Spirit's work.

Spiritual disciplines: Scripture meditation, journaling, breath prayer, attentiveness, truth telling

Week Four Group Discussion

1. Read Romans 12:18 together and discuss what it means to "live peaceably," "if it is possible," and "so far as it depends on you" (NRSV). What does true peacemaking require?

2. Without gossip, bitterness, or blame, share with one another any needs you have for prayer regarding relational conflicts or challenges.

3. Take turns reciting Psalm 23:1 around the circle. Allow for silence after each person recites the Scripture, asking God to reveal himself as the Good Shepherd who provides everything you need.

   "The LORD is my shepherd. I lack nothing."

Reading for Week Five:
Chapter Five

....

Week Five: Day One

∽

CHAPTER FIVE: *HANNAH* (PP. 115-118)

Scripture: Ecclesiastes 3:1-8

1. Nathan writes, "I'm praying for the gift of incarnational presence with
    your parents, Hannah, that you'll be empowered to meet them where
    they are and love them as they are without demanding anything else"
    (p. 115). What is the "gift of incarnational presence"? Have you ever re-
    ceived it? Offered it? What was that like for you?

2. How do you discern what kind of time it is? What role does community
    play in that process of discernment?

3. What does Hannah sense the Spirit calling her to do with regard to her
    parents? Does any part of her discernment resonate with you? Why or
    why not?

4. What is it time for you to forgive? To let go of?

5. Read Ecclesiastes 3:1-8 slowly, listening for words or phrases that catch your attention. What time is it? Offer what you notice to God in prayer.

. . . .

Week Five: Day Two

∞

CHAPTER FIVE: *HANNAH* (pp. 122-125, 130-132)

Scripture: Psalm 116:7

1. Nathan recommends that Hannah practice a new spiritual discipline with her friend: truth telling. Why is this hard for Hannah to do? Do you notice any patterns with Hannah and the way she interacts with others?

2. Which is easier for you, silence or speaking? Why?

3. In what ways has Hannah transposed her experiences as a "responsible child" onto her image of God? Do you share anything in common with her? Is there anything for you to release to God?

4. Think about false pictures you may have of God. What are the roots of these distorted images? What needs to be healed or transformed in the way you see God and yourself? Speak to God about this.

5. Read Psalm 116:7 several times, breathing it as prayer. In what ways has God dealt bountifully with you? Spend time rehearsing his goodness and offering gratitude. What do you notice about the restfulness of your soul after rehearsing God's faithfulness?

....

Week Five: Day Three

CHAPTER FIVE: *MARA* (PP. 126-129, 133-136)

Scripture: Romans 8:1-2

1. While conflict escalates with Brian, Mara is experiencing silence from God about how to manage him. She also is resisting setting up appointments with Katherine and Dawn. Why? What would you say to Mara if you were alongside her?

2. Read what Miss Jada offers to Mara (p. 134). What resonates with you as truth? In what ways do you get caught in a cycle of judgment and condemnation in the "shame and blame game"?

3. What does Miss Jada tell Mara to do? What if you were told these things? How would you respond?

4. Mara decides not to "burden" Meg with her stress. Do you agree with her decision? Why or why not?

5. Read Romans 8:1-2 several times. Offer your response to God in prayer.

··

Week Five: Day Four
∞

CHAPTER FIVE: *MEG AND HANNAH* (PP. 119-121, 137-140)

Scripture: Isaiah 11:6-9

1. Where does Meg go with her stress and heartache?

2. What do you notice about the way she processes her grief? The way she prays? Does she model anything for you?

3. The rabbit and the hawk incident becomes a parable for Meg about predators and prey. What's distressing her?

4. Write a "Dear Jesus" letter that honestly expresses your needs, hopes, and fears.

5. Read Isaiah 11:6-9 again, paying attention to words or images that stir your longings. Spend time praying for the kingdom to come in fullness.

....

Week Five: Day Five

CHAPTER FIVE: DISCERNMENT QUESTIONS

Scripture: James 1:5

1. Nate sends Hannah some questions adapted from St. Ignatius that help us discern the movement of the Spirit. Turn to page 131 and read the questions again. If you find yourself in a place of discernment, use these questions for prayer.

2. Meditate on James 1:5, trusting God to speak in a way you can hear and understand.

....

Week Five: Day Six

REVIEW

Review your notes from this week. Where are you invited to linger in prayer and reflection?

Spiritual disciplines: lament, Scripture meditation, forgiveness, discernment, self-examination, truth telling, prayer, gratitude

Week Five Group Discussion

1. Read Ecclesiastes 3:1-8 for group lectio divina. Share the words, phrases, and insights that came to life as you prayed.

2. Discuss your sympathies or frustrations, resonance or dissonance with the characters.

3. How can the group pray for you?

Reading for Week Six: Chapter Six

··

Week Six: Day One

∞

CHAPTER SIX: CHARISSA (PP. 141-146, 156-159)

Scripture: Ephesians 5:18-21

1. Describe the ongoing conflict in John and Charissa's marriage. Why are they both upset? Who do you identify with more easily? Why?

2. What do you notice about Charissa's preparations for welcoming her students? What about her interaction with them? If you were alongside her, what counsel would you give? How would you pray for her?

3. How willing are you to yield to the desires of others? Bring to mind any occasions when you were asked to submit your own plans out of love for someone else. How did you respond?

4. Read Ephesians 5:18-21 again. How might regular meditation on and practice of these commands affect the quality of your relationships? Offer your response to God in prayer.

Week Six: Day Two

CHAPTER SIX: MEDITATION ON ROMANS 8:31-39 (PP. 148-149)

Read the Scripture text and answer the personal reflection questions. You may need two days for these.

Week Six: Day Three

CHAPTER SIX: *MARA, MEG, AND HANNAH* (PP. 150-155)

Scripture: Romans 8:38-39

1. Mara, Meg, and Hannah each process their responses to the Romans 8 exercise. Do any of their reflections particularly resonate with you? If so, why?

2. Have you ever had an insight about your sin cause you pain? What was your response?

3. Have you ever had an experience of "resuscitated grief" overwhelm you? What was your response?

4. Are there any "I forgive you" or "Please forgive me" letters you're being called to write? To whom? If you aren't yet ready to write the letters, write down the names of the recipients.

5. In what ways is the Spirit shining light into dark places? How do you feel about what you see?

6. Read Romans 8:38-39 slowly. Offer your response to God in prayer.

....

Week Six: Day Four

∞

CHAPTER SIX: *HANNAH AND MARA* (PP. 160-168)

Scripture: Romans 8:31

1. Hannah prays, "Lord, it feels like too much abundance. Too much good. Like you have let me 'be full' and have 'all things.' And I don't know how to say thank you. I feel like I'm sitting beneath an overflowing cup, and I don't have the capacity to take it all in. So, Lord, enlarge my cup to receive your fullness so that everything I offer others comes out of the abundance I've received" (p. 163). Does this prayer reflect your life with God right now? If so, in what ways? If not, offer your own honest prayer.

2. While Hannah is experiencing abundant joy and a cup overflowing with goodness, Mara is experiencing anxiety over Jeremy and wrath from Tom. With which character do you most identify right now? Why?

3. If you were alongside both Hannah and Mara, how would you pray for each of them?

4. Read Romans 8:31 again. Offer your honest response to God.

....

Week Six: Day Five

⌒

CHAPTER SIX: MEDITATION ON ROMANS 8:31-39

Return to any unanswered questions or any that need further reflection in light of what's stirring for you this week.

....

Week Six: Day Six

⌒

REVIEW

Review your notes from this week. Is there a forgiveness letter for you to write? Any aha moments to further process?

Spiritual disciplines: Scripture meditation, breath prayer, forgiveness, gratitude, attentiveness, lament, submission, journaling, silence, self-examination, confession, community

Week Six Group Discussion

Turn to the Romans 8:31-39 exercise (pp. 148-149), read the Scripture together, and answer the group reflection questions.

Reading for Week Seven: Chapters Seven and Eight

Week Seven: Day One

CHAPTER SEVEN: MEG (PP. 169-173)

Scripture: Psalm 102:1-6

1. While Meg struggles to find a way forward with her sister, Hannah offers her a gift of sisterly love. Offer thanks to God for the sisters and brothers he has given you in Christ. Who has loved you well?

2. What do you notice about the emails Meg writes? Would you have sent an email to Becca? Why or why not?

3. Spend some time praying the Serenity Prayer by Reinhold Niebuhr. Which lines grab your attention? Challenge you? Comfort you?

    God, give us grace to accept with Serenity the things that cannot be changed, Courage to change the things which should be changed, and the Wisdom to distinguish the one from the other. Living one day at a time, enjoying one moment at a time, accepting hardship as a pathway to peace, taking, as Jesus did, this sinful world as it is, not as I would have it, trusting that You will make all things right, if I surrender to Your will, so that I may be reasonably happy in this life and supremely happy with You forever in the next. Amen.

4. Rehearse the things that do not have the power to separate you from God's love.

5. Read Psalm 102:1-6 aloud several times. Which words or phrases catch your attention? Why? Using images from Psalm 102, write your own prayer to express your longings, heartaches, needs, or fears.

....

Week Seven: Day Two

CHAPTER SEVEN: *CHARISSA* (PP. 174-179)

Scripture: Matthew 5:38-42

1. Charissa mentally compares and contrasts Wayfarer with First Church. What is she critical of? What is most likely to distract you in worship and cause you to become critical?

2. Hannah describes the spiritual formation class on the Sermon on the Mount as "open heart surgery without anesthetic sometimes, but good" (p. 175). When have you experienced spiritual open heart surgery? Do you welcome the Spirit's surgical work or dread it? Why?

3. Charissa recoils at Emily's use of the phrase "church-shopping." What do you think Charissa means when she mentally objects to being a "vulgar consumer of religious commodities"?

4. What does the "invitation to the cruciform life" look like for you? Where are you being "pressed into the likeness of Christ"? Called to die to self or walk the narrow way?

5. What comes to life for Charissa as she prayerfully listens to the Word being read? Do you identify with her wrestling?

6. Read Matthew 5:38-42 using lectio divina. Which words or phrases arrest you and invite you to ponder and pray? Offer what you notice to God.

....

Week Seven: Day Three

CHAPTER SEVEN: *HANNAH* (PP. 180-182)

Scripture: Matthew 5:38-42

1. What conflicts is Hannah battling? How do you navigate hurt feelings or disagreements?

2. Why is Matthew 5:38-42 a particularly challenging passage for Hannah to study? Do you share anything in common with her?

3. What painful truth does she see as she ponders her reasons why she poured herself out in serving others? Are there any surgical words for you in her revelation? Offer your response to God in prayer.

4. Sit with the paradigm shift Hannah describes. What does it mean to be converted from scarcity to abundance? How would this shift impact you?

5. Where are you being invited to stand barefoot, literally or figuratively, as a declaration of being on holy ground?

6. Read Matthew 5:38-42 again. Offer what you notice to God in prayer.

....

Week Seven: Day Four

CHAPTER SEVEN: *MARA AND CHARISSA* (PP. 183-188)

Scripture: James 2:15-17

1. Enter into Mara's emotions at the check-out counter. Have you ever experienced or witnessed something similar? How did you respond?

2. When Mara flings open her front door, she expects to find more judgment from a neighbor. Instead, she's startled by grace. Have you ever been surprised by generosity? Spend some time thanking God for the people who have been his messengers in times of need.

3. Charissa experiences the joy of giving. "Walking that extra mile had never been so invigorating. Ever" (p. 188). When have you had the opportunity to give generously to someone? What was that experience like for you?

4. Who stands beside you when you're suffering? Who is God calling you to stand alongside?

5. Read James 2:15-17 again. In what ways are you challenged or inspired by these words? What is your response?

Week Seven: Day Five

CHAPTER EIGHT: *HANNAH, MEG, AND CHARISSA* (PP. 189-205)

Scripture: 1 John 3:16-18

1. Hannah realizes after talking with Steve that "her determination to protect her privacy had only complicated the matter" (p. 193). Have you ever had a similar experience of needing to tell the whole truth after trying to conceal it? What was that like for you?

2. After getting an update from Hannah about her trip to the bank with Mara, Meg comments, "I've never really hated anyone before, but between Simon and Tom . . . well, I can't say I haven't fantasized about both of them getting what they deserve" (p. 196). What about you? Is there anyone you wish would receive judgment rather than mercy? Offer your thoughts and feelings to God in prayer.

3. What is Charissa's attitude toward her students? When are you tempted to show "zero tolerance" for someone?

4. In the middle of an evening of reminiscing about her wedding and honeymoon, Meg receives a phone call from her doctor that changes

everything. Have you ever received news that terrified you? How did you respond? Did anyone support you in this? Speak to God about what you remember or what you need.

5. Read 1 John 3:16-18 several times aloud, letting the words penetrate you. When have you loved only in word or speech? Where is God calling you to lay down your life for another and love in truth and action? How will you respond?

....

Week Seven: Day Six

REVIEW

Return to the questions or themes that challenged or stirred you this week. What action steps is God calling you to take?

Spiritual disciplines: corporate worship, lectio divina, serving, generosity, sacrifice, gratitude, community, journaling, study, self-examination, confession

Week Seven Group Discussion

1. Use Matthew 5:38-42 as a text for group lectio divina, then share what you noticed as you prayed.

2. What practical needs do the members of your group have? How can you generously serve one another?

3. What practical needs are there in your community? How can you generously serve together?

Reading for Week Eight: Chapter Nine

....

Week Eight: Day One

CHAPTER NINE: *HANNAH AND CHARISSA* (PP. 209-216)

Scripture: Romans 8:35-39

1. As Hannah waits for news, she plans ways to love and support Meg. When someone you love is suffering, how do you try to help? What gifts have been most important for you to receive when you've suffered? Why?

2. Hannah finds it difficult to know what to say to God in prayer. What words or phrases from her journal entry catch your attention? Why?

3. In what ways is Charissa wrestling? Do you identify with her struggle? Why or why not?

4. Look again at the way Hannah prays with Romans 8:35-39 in her journal entry (p. 213). Using words or images from Romans 8:35-39, write your own prayer. What are you convinced of?

....

Week Eight: Day Two

CHAPTER NINE: *MEG* (PP. 217-221)

Scripture: Psalm 6:1-6

1. Bring to mind some of the "ordinary moments that [make] up the fabric of ordinary, extraordinary lives" (p. 218). What memories are precious to you? Why? Spend time giving God thanks for these gifts.

2. David prays in Psalm 6:3, "My soul also is struck with terror, while you, O LORD—how long?" (NRSV). What words would you write after the dash? What is your prayer?

3. How practiced are you at praying the psalms of lament? Have they been your companions during times of sorrow, suffering, and trial? If so, which ones have been important to you? Why? If not, how might the prayers of anguish give words to your sighs and longings for yourself and others?

4. Meg returns to the exercise Katherine gave her in *Sensible Shoes*: personalizing verses from Isaiah 43. What do you need to hear from God right now?

5. Read Psalm 6:1-6 again. Then write your own prayer of lament. What do you need to say to God?

CHAPTER NINE: *ALL* (PP. 222-241)

Scripture: John 11:35

1. Each of the women is trying to process Meg's diagnosis in her own way. Do you identify with any of them? Why or why not?

2. What questions do you ask in the midst of suffering? What truths have been important for you to cling to? Why?

3. Are you able to tell Jesus, "I hurt"? Have a conversation with him about this.

4. Hannah journals about an experience of hearing an echoing verse and wondering what it had to do with her anguish over Meg (p. 240). What does it mean for you to fix your eyes on the cross of Jesus Christ and behold the Lamb of God, who takes away the sin of the world?

5. Hannah writes, "Even as I fix my eyes there, I hear my own soul chafe that it's not enough. I want you to end the pain now. I want you to reveal your glory now." Are you able to express your dissatisfaction honestly to God? Why or why not? Talk with God about this.

6. "Jesus wept" (John 11:35). What do these words mean to you? Offer your response to God in prayer.

··

Week Eight: Days Four and Five

CHAPTER NINE: *CHARISSA* (PP. 242-244)

Use the meditation on Psalm 90:12 (*Memento Mori*) in the Further Resources section of the book for your reflection and prayer.

··

Week Eight: Day Six

REVIEW

Prayerfully review your reflections from this week. What do you notice?

Spiritual disciplines: lament, journaling, service, intercession, Scripture meditation, community, self-examination, confession, gratitude

Week Eight Group Discussion

Use the meditation on Psalm 90:12 (*Memento Mori*) at the end of *Barefoot* to shape your time together.

Reading for Week Nine:
Chapter Ten

....

Week Nine: Day One

∞

CHAPTER TEN: *MEG AND HANNAH* (PP. 245-253)

Scripture: Romans 13:11

1. With Hannah's intervention, Meg finally has an opportunity to speak with Becca and give her the news. How would you have responded to Becca if you were Hannah? Meg? If any memories from your own life are stirred, offer what you notice to God in prayer.

2. Hannah uses discernment questions (see p. 131) to pray about the timing of the wedding. Do any of her ponderings and realizations resonate with you? Why or why not?

3. What is the difference between *chronos* and *kairos* time? What kind of time are you most aware of? What would it mean to become more aware of *kairos* moments in the midst of *chronos*?

4. Read Romans 13:11 slowly and prayerfully, keeping in mind that the Greek word for *time* in this verse is *kairos*. In what ways is God quickening and awakening you? Offer your response to God in prayer.

Week Nine: Day Two

CHAPTER TEN: MARA (PP. 254-259, 265-269)

Scripture: Mark 11:25

1. What do you make of Mara's first response to the news about Tom's pregnant girlfriend? What about her later response as she walks Bailey in the park? In what ways do you identify with her progression of emotions as she processes the news?

2. Do you think Mara should have mailed the letter to Tess? Why or why not?

3. What do you notice about the series of letters to Tom that Mara writes and shreds? Are there any letters for you to write, send, or shred?

4. Do you recognize any resistance within yourself regarding asking for or offering forgiveness? How might seeing the resistance be progress? What next step is God calling you to take?

5. Slowly and prayerfully read Mark 11:25 again. Do you have anything against anyone? Are you willing to begin the process of forgiveness? Offer your response to God in prayer.

....

Week Nine: Day Three

CHAPTER TEN: *HANNAH* (PP. 260-264)

Scripture: James 1:5-6

1. Which details catch your attention from Hannah's conversation with Steve? If you were Hannah, what would you be concerned about?

2. In what ways does Hannah see that her pride is wrapped up in her reaction? In what ways do you identify with her?

3. Have you ever made a decision and then panicked or second-guessed it? Bring to mind the details and talk with God about the outcome.

4. What does it mean for you to "heartily yield all things" to God's "pleasure and disposal"? Offer both your willingness and resistance to God in prayer.

5. Read James 1:5-6 slowly and prayerfully several times, listening for a word or phrase that catches your attention and invites you to linger. What is your prayer?

....

Week Nine: Day Four

CHAPTER TEN: *CHARISSA AND MEG* (PP. 270-273)

Scripture: Galatians 6:2

1. What assumptions does Charissa make about her students? What assumptions are you quick or prone to make about others? Why?

2. What gifts is Charissa able to offer her student? What gifts do you have that might bring relief and help to someone who is suffering?

3. Meg decides to have a brave and direct conversation with Hannah about what she wants and needs. What helps you to be brave in declaring what you want and need?

4. Is there anyone God is calling you to have a loving, honest conversation with? Spend some time listening in prayer.

5. Slowly and prayerfully read Galatians 6:2. What burdens are you being called to help carry? In what ways does love "fulfill the law of Christ"? Offer your response to God in prayer.

....

Week Nine: Day Five

CHAPTER TEN: *MEG* (PP. 274-276)

Scripture: John 19:23-27

1. Meg has resisted spending time meditating on the crucifixion because it's too sad, cruel, gruesome, and disturbing for her to imagine. What about you? Offer any resistance to God in prayer.

2. Katherine suggested that Meg use her imagination to ponder the cross: "Watch for his love." What helps you watch for Jesus' love?

3. What details from Meg's prayer of imagination catch your attention? Why?

4. Read John 19:23-27 again and imagine that you are at the foot of the cross, either as an observer or as one of Jesus' named loved ones. Pay attention to the thoughts and emotions that are stirred within you as you watch the events unfold and as you listen to Jesus speak. Offer what you notice to God in prayer.

· ·

Week Nine: Day Six

∞

REVIEW

Prayerfully review your notes for the week. What action steps are you being called to take?

Spiritual disciplines: discernment, community, breath prayer, seeking and offering forgiveness, service, truth telling, journaling, praying with imagination, self-examination, confession

Week Nine Group Discussion

1. Open your session by reading John Wesley's prayer (p. 52). Then discuss which lines are most difficult for you to pray and why.

2. Share your reflections about letters or conversations you feel called to pursue. Pray for one another for wisdom and discernment.

3. Either pray with imagination together using John 19:23-27 or take time to share what you noticed as you prayed with the text.

Reading for Week Ten: Chapter Eleven

Week Ten: Day One

∞

CHAPTER ELEVEN: *HANNAH* (PP. 277-280)

Scripture: Luke 24:50-51

1. Hannah isn't sure whether she's living in denial or faith. How can you tell the difference between them? What's the evidence of denial? The evidence of faith?

2. Katherine invites Nathan and Hannah to speak openly and honestly about their fears and struggles and to name the deaths and losses in order to also name the resurrection and new life. Spend some time naming to God your fears, struggles, losses, deaths, and disequilibrium. Then spend time naming to God the points of resurrection and new life you see in light of what has changed or died.

3. Hannah ponders Jesus' words to Mary Magdalene: "Do not cling to me" (John 20:17 ESV). In her journal she writes, "If we don't let go of what has been, there can be no ascension to new life. So, do not cling to what

has been or even to what is, but always be willing to let it go" (p. 280). What do you cling to? What are you being invited to let go of?

4. How might you practice beholding the cross of Christ as the deepest evidence of the love of God? How might you practice beholding the empty tomb as evidence of God's power and faithfulness?

5. Read Luke 24:50-51 slowly and prayerfully, imagining that you are standing with the disciples as Jesus ascends and gives his blessing. What thoughts and emotions stir within you? Offer what you notice to God in prayer.

....

Week Ten: Day Two

CHAPTER ELEVEN: MARA (PP. 281-283, 301-303)

Scripture: Romans 12:14-21

1. Name some of the thoughts and emotions Mara is aware of as she talks with Jeremy at Charissa's house. In what ways do you identify with her?

2. Jeremy would love for Tom to suffer and wonders if he can pray for that. How does Mara respond? What is stirred in you by her response?

3. What's your reaction to Tess's letter to Jeremy? Do you think Mara did the right thing in writing and sending the letter to Tess? Why or why not?

4. If you were Mara, how would you respond to Tess now? Why?

5. Slowly read Romans 12:14-21 aloud. Which words or phrases catch your attention? Provoke you? Where do you notice your own resistance? Offer what you notice to God in prayer.

....

Week Ten: Day Three

CHAPTER ELEVEN: MEG (PP. 284-287, 294-297)

Scripture: Colossians 3:12-13

1. What details from Meg's forgiveness letter to her mother catch your attention? Why? Is there any letter you're being called to write? *Will you, beloved?*

2. The image of the bare and twisted tree continues to speak to Meg about being resilient in hope. What images speak to you about being resilient in hope? Why?

3. If you were Meg, how would you respond to Simon traveling with Becca and the plans they've already made together? What emotions would rise within you? Have you ever had a similar experience with disappointment and anger? Offer what you notice to God in prayer.

4. Read Colossians 3:12-13 again. Ask the Spirit to shine light into dark places of bitterness, blame, or resentment. Do you have anything against anyone? Respond to God in prayer.

5. Is there a forgiveness letter for you to write? Begin or continue the process.

....

Week Ten: Day Four

CHAPTER ELEVEN: *CHARISSA AND HANNAH* (PP. 288-293, 298-300)

Scripture: Matthew 16:24-25

1. Charissa and John are celebrating and looking forward to their future with joy and hope. What are you celebrating? What are you grateful for? Offer what you notice to God in prayer.

2. Hannah is confronted with her own selfishness, deceit, and immaturity when Nancy reacts to her news with anger and hurt. How do you feel when you see your sin? Talk with God about this.

3. Nate reminds Hannah that "shock over our own sin is a manifestation of pride, a love of our own excellence," and he asks her whether she's more upset about Nancy's hurt or her own faults (p. 290). Is there anything for you to take to heart in Nate's words? What would it mean for you to confess your sins rather than be surprised or chagrined by them?

4. After hearing the rumors that are circulating about her at Westminster, Hannah ponders what it means to let her reputation as a devoted, faithful servant die (pp. 293, 299-300). Have you ever had to die to how other people view you? What does it mean for you to keep company with Jesus in the face of false accusations? Offer your own struggle to God in prayer.

5. What does "dying to self" mean? In what ways is God calling you to die? Which deaths are hardest for you? Why?

6. Read Matthew 16:24-25 again several times. Which words or phrases catch your attention and call for your response?

....

Week Ten: Day Five

∞

CHAPTER ELEVEN: *MEG* (PP. 304-306)

Scripture: 1 Corinthians 15:51-55

1. Despite Meg watching for openings for deep and meaningful conversation with Becca, Becca is more comfortable having mother-daughter fun together. If you were Meg, what would you do? Have you ever found yourself in a similar situation? What did you do?

2. Ponder the transformation process from caterpillar to butterfly. Which images catch your attention and speak to you? Why?

3. Where do you find yourself in the process of transformation? Frantic to be free? Exhausted by the rigor? Waiting to fly? Overturned and helpless? Experiencing the joy of freedom? Spend time journaling your response.

4. Pray for others who are enduring the mystery and rigor of transformation. Who can you be alongside to encourage and cheer on?

5. Read 1 Corinthians 15:51-55 again. Which words or phrases catch your attention and invite your meditation and prayer?

....

Week Ten: Day Six

REVIEW

Return to any questions you didn't have the opportunity to consider prayerfully. What are your most significant insights or challenges from the week?

Spiritual disciplines: Scripture meditation, praying with imagination, lament, truth telling, forgiveness, journaling, self-examination, confession, silence, gratitude, celebration, spiritual direction

Week Ten Group Discussion

1. Choose one of the Scripture texts from this week and practice group lectio divina. Then share what you noticed as you listened and prayed. How is the Spirit revealing Jesus? Enlarging you? Transforming you into his likeness?

2. Discuss the theme of "dying to self" and talk about ways the characters are being called to die. In what ways are you being called to die? Which deaths are most difficult for you to embrace? Why?

3. Share any other moments of insight from your prayer and reflection times this week. Close by praying for one another.

Reading for Week Eleven: Chapters Twelve and Thirteen

Note: If you are using this guide with a group, plan to have a basin, bowl, and towel available for foot washing when you meet together.

....

Week Eleven: Day One

CHAPTERS TWELVE AND THIRTEEN:
HANNAH, CHARISSA, AND MEG (PP. 307-322)

Scripture: Song of Solomon 6:3

1. What are some of the gifts of love the characters are receiving and offering? What gifts of love are you receiving and offering? Spend time thanking God for these.

2. Name some of the trials and disappointments they are experiencing. Are there any particular struggles you identify with? Offer what you notice to God in prayer.

3. What spiritual disciplines help you meditate on the love of God?

4. "I am my beloved's and my beloved is mine" (Song of Solomon 6:3). Match these words to your breathing, inhaling the first phrase and exhaling the second phrase. Use this as your breath prayer this week.

....

Week Eleven: Day Two

∞

CHAPTER THIRTEEN: MEDITATION ON
JOHN 13:1-15, 21 (PP. 323-324)

Slowly read the text a couple of times, imagining yourself in the upper room. Then journal your responses to the personal reflection questions.

....

Week Eleven: Day Three

∞

CHAPTER THIRTEEN: *MARA AND HANNAH*
(PP. 325-327)

Scripture: John 13:12-15

1. Which details of Mara's prayer of imagination catch your attention? Why?

2. Which details of Hannah's journal entry catch your attention? Why?

3. What does "dying to self" mean for you today? Whose feet are you being called to wash? How do you feel about this? Talk with God about it.

4. Read John 13:12-15 again, listening for a word or phrase that catches your attention and invites your meditation and prayer. What is your response?

....

Week Eleven: Day Four

CHAPTER THIRTEEN: *MEG* (PP. 328-333)

Scripture: Song of Solomon 2:10-12

1. What gifts of love do Meg and Becca give to one another? Which ones speak deeply to you? Why?

2. Have you ever experienced a "holy moment" like the one Meg describes with the mourning doves? If so, remember and savor the details.

3. In what ways is the Lover of your soul summoning you to himself? What is your response?

4. What does the promise of resurrection mean to you? What are some "defiant" symbols that remind you death does not have the final word?

5. Read Song of Solomon 2:10-12 again. Listen to the voice of the beloved speak these words to you: "Arise, my love, my beautiful one, and come away" (ESV). What is your response?

....

Week Eleven: Day Five

∽

CHAPTER THIRTEEN: MEDITATION
ON JOHN 13:1-15, 21 (PP. 323-324)

1. Slowly read the text a couple of times, imagining yourself in the upper room again. What do you notice this time? Has anything changed in your response to Jesus and to the others gathered in the room? Offer to God in prayer anything you notice about your receptivity or resistance.

2. What next steps will you take to love and serve someone in Jesus' name?

....

Week Eleven: Day Six

∽

REVIEW

Prayerfully review your notes from this week. What are your most significant insights or challenges?

Spiritual disciplines: Scripture meditation, community, praying with imagination, journaling, service, submission, generosity, forgiveness, foot washing, breath prayer, celebration, self-examination, confession

Week Eleven Group Discussion

Read John 13:1-15, 21 and imagine yourselves in the upper room together. Then discuss your responses to the group reflection questions, offering either insights from your prayer with this text earlier in the week or something new that arises now as you pray.

After you pray for one another, conclude your time together by washing one another's feet.

Reading for Week Twelve:
Chapter Fourteen

....

Week Twelve: Day One

CHAPTER FOURTEEN: *HANNAH AND MEG* (PP. 334-341)

Scripture: Matthew 5:4

1. Which details from the last dinner together catch your attention? Why?

2. Have you ever had an opportunity to share a last word, blessing, or benediction with a loved one? What was that experience like for you?

3. Are there any words of blessing or benediction that you still have an opportunity to speak to someone? What might God call you to say?

4. What promises from God's Word would be most comforting to hear in your last hours? Why?

5. Read Matthew 5:4 again several times. In what ways has this beatitude been true in your life? What do you mourn right now? How is God comforting you? Spend time receiving the blessing of God's comfort in the midst of sorrow.

....

Week Twelve: Day Two

∞

CHAPTER FOURTEEN: *HANNAH, CHARISSA, AND MARA* (PP. 342-348)

Scripture: 1 Corinthians 15:3-4

1. Name some of the gifts the characters are receiving and offering. Which ones speak to you? Why?

2. If you were to write your own funeral service right now, which Scriptures, songs, or readings would you want to include? What do you hope would be said about you?

3. Hannah writes, "Here I am, Lord, in the garden of my heart, surrendering longings and desires to you. Again" (p. 346). Recall some painful

moments of relinquishment in your own life. How did God meet you? Is there anything you're being asked to lay down now? Talk with God about what you notice.

4. What encouragement have you received about the progress you're making in your life with God? What words of encouragement would help you move forward with hope? What words of hope are you handing on to others?

5. Read 1 Corinthians 15:3-4 several times, listening for a word or phrase that captures your attention and invites your prayerful pondering. Offer what you notice to God in prayer.

....

Week Twelve: Day Three

Chapter Fourteen: Hannah (PP. 349-355)

Scripture: John 11:25-26

1. Hannah tells Becca that her mother was brave. How do you define *brave*? Who do you know who is brave? Speak to God about your responses.

2. Spend some time meditating and praying with these stanzas from *Christ the Lord Is Risen Today* by Charles Wesley (1739). (You may also wish to look up the entire hymn to pray with.)

    > Lives again our glorious King; Alleluia!
    > Where, O death, is now thy sting? Alleluia!
    > Once he died, our souls to save; Alleluia!
    > Where thy victory, O grave? Alleluia!

    > Soar we now where Christ has led; Alleluia!
    > Following our exalted Head; Alleluia!
    > Made like him, like him we rise; Alleluia!
    > Ours the cross, the grave, the skies. Alleluia!

3. What helps you to remember and rehearse the joy of resurrection in the midst of searing loss?

4. Where are you being invited to take off your shoes and worship God on holy ground?

5. Read John 11:25-26 again. Imagine standing face to face with Jesus as he speaks these words to you. *Do you believe this?* Have an honest conversation with God about your trust and confidence in these promises.

Week Twelve:
Days Four, Five, and Six

TWELVE-WEEK REVIEW

Prayerfully read over your notes from the past three months. What catches your attention? What encourages you? What are you mourning? What are you celebrating? What next steps will you take?

Spiritual disciplines: service, sacrifice, breath prayer, Scripture meditation, lament, celebration, community, praying with hymn lyrics, the ministry of encouragement and comfort, journaling, gratitude

Week Twelve Group Discussion

1. Open by reading Hebrews 10:24-25 in unison: "And let us consider how we may spur one another on toward love and good deeds, not giving up meeting together, as some are in the habit of doing, but encouraging one another—and all the more as you see the Day approaching."

2. Discuss what it means to "spur one another on toward love and good deeds." How have you been able to do this during your journey together? What next steps can you take as a group?

3. Share any significant insights from your reading and reflections this week.

4. Spend time offering words of encouragement to one another (*eulogy* means "good word"), taking turns to savor and receive these good words.

5. Close your time together by removing your shoes and praying together, using this blessing from Numbers 6:24-26 (NRSV) as your closing benediction:

   The LORD bless you and keep you;
   the LORD make his face to shine upon you, and be gracious to you;
   the LORD lift up his countenance upon you, and give you peace.

The Sensible Shoes Series

Sensible Shoes
Two Steps Forward
Barefoot
An Extra Mile

STUDY GUIDES

For more information about the Sensible Shoes series,
visit ivpress.com/sensibleshoesseries.
To learn more from Sharon Garlough Brown or to sign up for her newsletter,
go to ivpress.com/sharon-news.